The Amazon Diary

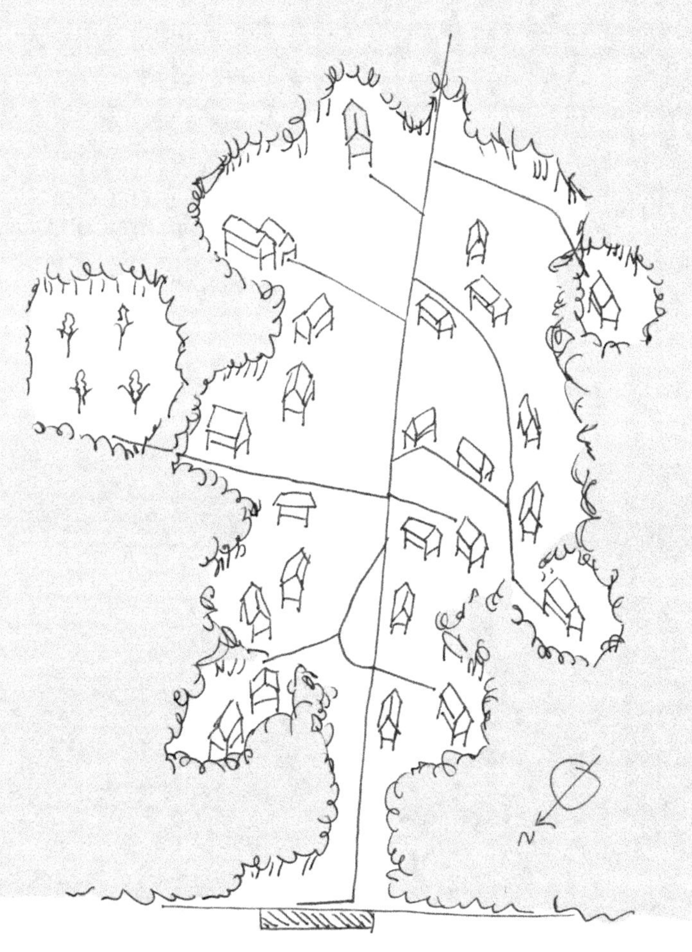

rivier

THE AMAZON DIARY

Elzo Smid

NUR: 302
ISBN: 9789083055978

At Jorge Chávez airport in Lima, I have to wait at least three hours for the domestic flight to Puerto Maldonado. I already read the documentation provided by our office staff on the plane and bought a notebook at an airport kiosk to take notes. It will be some time before I reach my final destination. This then is day 1 of my Peru adventure.

Two weeks ago I had a meeting with Rob Kluytmans, my superior. I was fifteen minutes early at the conference room on the top floor of the Rotterdam headquarters. That room depresses me big time, the wooden panels on the wall, the bulbous lamps above the enormous table. It smells of the cigars and cigarettes smoked there days before. Clearly the 1970s have still not made their influence felt there.
While waiting, I looked out over the city through the glass wall. In the distance was the harbor. There had been an article in the newspaper about the new container crane on the quay. Containers had been coming into the harbor for years, but now there was a special crane on the quayside for them. A logistical revolution in the harbor. I think more container cranes will follow.

Fortunately, I get along well with Rob; I regard him as a friend rather than a boss. We have known each other for a long time and Gonny was friends with his wife. Often, when one of us had their birthday, the four of us would go out and have dinner together, on a weekend or at the moment I returned from abroad. They were also a support to me when Gonny passed away. In terms of work, Rob kept me on the sidelines for over a year, but now the time has come for another trip abroad.

It's all about the Brazil nuts, he told me. Our company uses them in chocolate bars, in granola and in trail mix. In those, they are not the main ingredient, but they are the biggest nuts. We also use the flour and oil of the Brazil nut. The oil, for example, is used in hair lotion, conditioner, and in soap and skin care products.

The nuts grow in the Amazon forest, especially in Brazil. But we import them from Peru, because the infrastructure is better there and the supply more reliable. The nuts have a hard shell that is removed in Spain. So we import them in their shells from Peru to Europe.

The problem is that the EEC *) will have stricter rules on nut imports next year. The shells may develop a fungus, *Aspergillus flavus,* that produces aflatoxin. And that substance is probably carcinogenic. The permissible amount of fungus is limited, and that limit is going down drastically. By the way, the same goes for other nuts such as almonds and hazelnuts, even dried fruits, corn, and rice.

It is up to me to see what can be done about this regarding the Brazil nuts. Spray them with a fungicide? Irradiate them with

*) *European Economic Community, the forerunner of the European Union*

ultraviolet light? Heat them? And at what stage of the whole process? Or should something completely different be done?
I am looking forward to it and hope to find the solution soon. My return flight has not been booked yet, but I expect to finish my research in Peru after two or three weeks and deliver my full report a few weeks later.

May 9, 1978

One other thing. I asked Rob who the contact person at the plantation was. He told me, to my surprise, that there are no plantations. All Brazil nuts grow in the wild. Every Brazil nut in our product, every nut in the supermarket has been harvested by farming families in the Amazon forest. During a period of about three months after the rainy season. Our contacts are employees of Planeta Peru, the *acopiador,* who buy the nuts from the farmers.

This is my third day in Puerto Maldonado. This morning I was given a tour of the processing plants.
Burlap sacks, filled with nuts from the jungle, are transported from the jungle by long boats across the river. On the shore, these are manually lifted onto a small kind of train that runs

from the river along a track steeply up the shore to the warehouses. It resembles the kind of carts like those used in mines. The process that follows is not very interesting: weighing the sacks, sampling the nuts, paying the seller, and then taking the sacks into storage.

The giant piles of sacks in the large wooden warehouses are impressive. I find it hard to imagine that they are all filled with shelled nuts from the surrounding jungle.

Of course I asked why there are no plantations, why every Brazil nut is harvested in the wild. I was invited to lunch so they could tell me all about it.

It appears that there have been several attempts to grow Brazil nut trees on plantations, both in Peru and Brazil, but so far they have all failed. There are several reasons for this. It takes fifteen to twenty-five years for a tree to produce its first nuts and as many as forty years to reach its maximum yield. So a plantation would be a huge investment; at least fifteen years of nurturing before even a penny is earned.

But the most important reason is pollination. After all, without pollination, the tree does not produce nuts. And that's a complicated story.

The flowers of the Brazil nut tree are large and plump. Nectar and pollen sit behind a spherical hatch, and there is only one kind of insect strong enough to get past that: the orchid bee. And even then, only the females. (I will try to draw it as soon as I find a dead bee.)

Firstly, the orchid bee is attracted not by the flowers of the Brazil nut tree, but by the orchids that live on the branches of the tree, the so-called *epiphytes.* Only the males, the drones, are attracted by the scent of these flowers. A complex composition of aromatic substances in these orchids causes the wings of the males to change color. This, in turn, attracts the females. These are larger than the males and have longer tongues. They eventually provide the pollination of the Brazil nut tree. When all these factors are in place, it still takes another 14 months for ripe Brazil nuts to fall from the tree.

On plantations, the situation cannot be replicated in such a way that the epiphytes will live on the branches. So the orchid bees don't show up, the trees are not pollinated and no nuts will grow.

I marvel at this complicated collaboration, this fragile balance, on which the entire Brazil nut harvest depends.

Today was a quiet day. I had a walk through the town and had some food and drinks on the patio of a small café. Fantastic coffee they have here. The owner told me that the beans are grown some 250 miles from here. On the cold mountain plateaus, which results in a different sugar content.

I noticed again that I really am a stranger here. Everyone has olive-brown skin and jet-black hair (unless it's gray) and is at least a head shorter than myself, at over 6 feet. And people are more thickly dressed, even though the atmosphere is quite warm, dry and almost windless. The smell of burned garbage hangs in the air.

Puerto Maldonado lies on the border of the Peruvian lowlands and the Amazon jungle. Here the Tambopata River joins the Madre de Dios after which it flows as an even wider river into the jungle. This also makes it the gateway for everyone to the Peruvian part of the Amazon forest.

Almost all buildings in the city are one-story, very occasionally you see a store or garage with an extra level of housing above it. Only in the downtown area are a few offices and government buildings of three or four stories. The dirt roads are wide, ochre-colored, dusty and full of mopeds and tuk-tuks. They typically have a median strip, a strip of grass with bushes and trees.

There are a lot of green spaces everywhere. There is also a scattering of tropical trees, reminding you of the jungle nearby.

The streets and buildings seem poorly maintained, but that is mostly deceptive and is mainly due to the climate, with part of the year temperatures of over 95 °F, and another part of the year torrential rains. Even my hotel looks shabby from the outside while inside everything is beyond reproach.

The old downtown area, near the point where the rivers meet, has a square, *Plaza de Armas* with a small bell tower in the middle. Oddly enough, the tower has been built on piles, as if to reflect the pile dwellings in the villages along the river.
Tomorrow I will go into the jungle and visit a village of *castañeros*, families who harvest Brazil nuts after each rainy season.

May 11, 1978

I am on my way to Iyacu, the village of the farming families that harvest the nuts. In a covered taxi boat with a small outboard motor, against the current, chugging along the Rio Tambopata. The boat is stable and the river is smooth as glass, so I can write undisturbed without the words becoming illegible.

This way we glide along the water into the jungle, but most of all it feels like leaving the city and leaving behind the world of noise, dust and stench, the music, mopeds and aggregates.
Near the big city the river was so wide that it looked more like a lake. With some small scattered houses and fields on the shore. Further ahead, the river becomes slightly narrower, but even so I estimate it at 1000 to 1300 feet wide. Here, too, the river is shallow, and the man at the helm has to skillfully avoid the sandbanks.
On the river bank, some dirt tracks can be seen at first. They run parallel to the river, a few yards away from it and with a thin strip of trees and shrubs in between, but after a while those tracks have also disappeared.
I am overwhelmed by the relative peace and quiet here. I see a huge light-brown plain, with the dense jungle on either side and the occasional small pile dwellings, or a few boats on a small stretch of river beach. Of course I feast my eyes, but sometimes I doze off a bit and only look up when the "captain" points something out to me, like a swimming family of capybaras, the largest rodents in the world.

Before going to the boat, I first had to go through a small building that sort of holds the middle between a customs house and a retail store. There they checked my clothes and the other stuff I was carrying to see what was redundant and what was lacking. The things that were lacking I could still buy on the spot. Redundant clothing stays behind in one of the special lockers with a note attached to it specifying my name and the date by which it will be picked up again.

Everything is done in very good spirits, and the prices are also reasonable. It's a good service, and it's to prevent me from carrying unnecessary stuff or suddenly realizing I'm in need of something in the jungle later on.

So now I am on my way, fully equipped, completely ready for the rainforest. The only luxuries I still carry are the watch on my wrist and the necklace with locket around my neck. The lid, with Gonny's portrait behind it, opens with difficulty.

May 15, 1978

My first visit to the village was short and all we did was make some arrangements. Yesterday was my second visit. I asked the villagers where the nearest Brazil nut tree was. I had seen the nuts and their processing in the city, but I now wanted to visit the source. They described an easy route to a slightly higher area and told me it would be by far the tallest tree there. I was given a hard hat and a machete to take along. A machete sounds aggressive, but it is pure necessity if you want to get a move on through the jungle. Even though there are tracks, each time new plants will have grown there and branches will be hanging over the tracks.

Tambopata is both the name of the river and the area around it. It seems that *tambo* is the Quechua word for "building" and that *pata* means "high ground".

Finding one's orientation here is not done with the directions of the compass, but by referring to upstream or downstream and the distance to the river. The river meanders a lot, so this can be pretty confusing at times.

On the river and in the village, you can tell where east or west is by the position of the sun, but in the jungle with its dense canopy, it is of no use. A compass is useless because the trunks of some tree species contain so much iron that they cause interference with any compass.

After a short walk through the forest, I arrive at the area that was described to me. It is an elevation surrounded by a horseshoe-shaped lake, a remnant of the meandering river. I immediately see the giant straight trunk topped by a crown that I can just barely see through the foliage several yards above all the other trees. But along the trunk and among the leaves I can also see dozens of large bulbs hanging like matt-brown bowling balls. What kind of tree is this? These are clearly not Brazil nuts. Did they send me to a different tree? Had I not been clear enough when I asked about it?

Surprised and disappointed, I look around. Then I see several of those cannonballs lying on the soggy soil. Most of them are open, as if scalped. Now I understand that Brazil nuts grow in these big globes, like seeds in a fruit. Fruit is an odd name

because the "shell", which is nearly an inch thick, is incredibly hard. When I hit it with the blunt side of the machete, it doesn't even make a dent and the sound is as if it's made of concrete.

While I'm examining the inside of a specimen, one of those cannonballs comes crashing down. Although the fall is audibly slowed by branches and leaves of smaller trees, it still makes a big dent in the soggy soil. So this explains the need for the hard hat.

So each nut as we know it is contained in two protective layers; each in its own shell and then collectively in the larger "fruit".
With my machete, I try to knock a piece off one of the hard fruits. I succeed after several attempts. I understand that gatherers use their machetes to get the nuts from the fruit, but how does that happen in nature? How does a nut become a new plant? How can the nuts ever take root if they are trapped in such a rock-hard ball?

Why wasn't this mentioned in the documentation I got from my company? Do they not know this? Do they only know the nuts as they are shelled in Spain, and do they have no idea how they actually grow?

In my mind I went back to the warehouses in Puerto Maldonado. Tens of thousands of Brazil nuts were lying there in huge piles of hundreds of burlap sacks. The nuts that are exported all over the world. Brazil nuts are among Peru's top five export products, along with timber, rubber and coffee.

A mature tree produces between 275 and 550 pounds of shelled nuts per year. This is an entire industry that depends on the Brazil nuts growing in the wild.

Back in the village, I first consult the documentation I got from my company. In it, no mention is made either of how a Brazil nut becomes a new tree. They are there, the young trees, but the link or links between the fallen bowling balls and the young plants is unknown.

If the emergence of new trees depends on unknown conditions, then these can change without us knowing it, with disastrous consequences for the industry. But apart from that industry, I wonder: how does nature do it?

I don't recall having ever encountered such a miraculous crop in all the years I've worked at the company. This is something I want to know more about.

I am able to spend a night in Iyacu. Many villages in this area have a Spanish name, after some saint or other, but this village has an indigenous (Guarayo, the Quechua dialect they speak here) name. I've been told it translates as "here" or "with us". The tribes living in this part of the forest call themselves Ese Eja, which simply means something like "people" or "nation".

It turns out that there is a vacant little wooden house at the very back of the village, against the edge of the jungle. A missionary, Padre Luís, used to live there, but he left posthaste. The villagers don't want to say much about it. An elderly couple manages the house and they have cleared it up for me. However, there is still a large wooden desk in the back of the house, which looks strange here in the jungle.

The couple said they have a son and daughter. The son, Tino, trying to find a job, left the village. Their daughter, Nina, they told with a proud smile, was the first from the village to study at the University of Cusco. It seems she is called "the jewel of the village".

The village is a large clearing in the dense forest, a grassy field with about thirty houses and a path leading to the river. As you go deeper into the forest behind the houses you, leave everything behind. The sounds take over. It is hot, humid and relatively dark; the foliage at various heights blocks almost all direct sunlight.

I find it beautiful and in a way soothing. But it is also over-whelming and disorienting; you smell the heat, hear the humidity, feel the almost complete shade.

And then there's the acoustics and "the orchestra", the layering of sounds that penetrate the thick foliage; the continuous buzzing and chirping of insects, the interludes of croaking frogs, the merry sounds of birds, and the occasional screech of a monkey sounding louder than the rest. This also varies depending on the time of day. Of course there is daytime and nighttime with, for example, frogs and bats after sunset. But the birds you hear in the morning are also different from those at the end of the day.

Entering the forest reminded me of the big tent during a boy-scouts' summer camp, the dim light, the humid air and the smell of grass, which oddly enough is stronger inside the tent, with its floor tarp, than outside.

May 20, 1978

Finally I found a good moment to ask the villagers about opening the fruit of the Brazil nut tree. They told me that there is an animal living in the jungle that can uniquely open the rock-hard fruit. They call it chiwayru (Guarayo) or agouti. Is it that simple? The agouti opens the big fruits and takes out the nuts?

What we know as Brazil nuts, I keep refering to as "nuts", even though they are actually seeds. In my mend I conveniently refer to the large nut as the "fruit", although that is an odd name for

something so hard. The respective Spanish names *castañas* and *cocos* are merely confusing.

The villagers call for Chico. He is a young man who knows most about the plants and animals in the jungle. He speaks Spanish and a little English. It turns out that he usually acts as a guide on the rare occasions when the village receives foreign visitors. He uses gestures to describe the agouti, a large rodent.

At the top of the fruit there is a hole where the stalk would be, much like with a citrus fruit that has its sepals removed. There the agouti begins to gnaw until it can open the large fruit and extract the nuts. After all that labor, the agouti strips the nuts of their shell and then, of course, it eats them. Chico demonstrated with squirrel-like gestures how the agouti eats a nut.
Apparently the nuts are still viable after they have left the body. Back home we know this, for example, from berries and seeds eaten by birds. There are even seeds that can germinate only after they have passed through the digestive tract of an animal. Is it really that simple? Then why was it always a mystery how new trees originate?

Just to be sure, I ask Chico if the agouti is a real animal rather than some kind of mythical creature. And whether he has ever seen them. Oh yes, he says laughing, countless times, they are as real as any other animal or plant in the forest. If I stay longer I will definitely see them myself, he assures me.

Does this mean that the tree depends on one large rodent that has to make a great effort to open the fruit and eat the nuts before new plants can grow? And on no other animal?

What happens if the agoutis find other kinds of nuts that are easier to open? What if they ignore the Brazil nuts? What if the agouti becomes extinct, does the tree then become extinct, too?

May 28, 1978

I cancelled the hotel in Puerto Maldonado and decided to stay some time in the old missionary home in Iyacu.

I will try to draw a plan of the village. It starts at the small jetty by the river. Then there is, perpendicular to the river, a path into the jungle. Most of the houses are situated on the edge of a bright green grassy field of irregular shape. Behind practically every building, the jungle begins. A few houses are situated a little deeper in the forest. Further along is a field where the villagers grow crops. On the grass some chickens walk around and two or three dogs that apparently have no owner.

The house I have moved into has virtually no walls. Two-thirds of it actually consists of a porch. In the back is a walled room where there is a bed and a large desk. The gable roof has a large tree trunk as its ridge beam, with long leaves on either side as roofing.

The bed in the room has a clean mattress and a new mosquito net. I carried out the desk with a couple of villagers. One of the bottom drawers had a lock and we couldn't find a key. So we broke it open. I was surprised to see that it contained only a handful of dead cockroaches. The others immediately started talking excitedly and looked angry. It is a method to make fake documents look older they told me. Usually these are forged title deeds or sales contracts of parcels of land; bits of jungle illegally seized for agriculture. A few days in a drawer full of cockroaches and the paper looks years older. What did Padre Luís have to do with that?

Behind the house, near the first trees of the forest, we found a metal fire-pit with burnt papers. There wasn't much left of them, but I could tell they had been magazines.

June 1, 1978

Of course, I still think of Gonny often. It is now over a year since I had to let her go.

I first met her during the parties in the harbor of Rotterdam. She attended those parties, she claimed, to practice her knowledge of foreign languages. At that time I was a cook on sea-going ships. In those days, when we stayed in foreign ports, I loved to visit the markets. For example, at times when circumstances forced the ship to stay longer so that supplies on board were getting insufficient.

Of course there were vendors on the wharf specialized in supplying the foreign ships, but I preferred to travel inland. Sometimes I even visited a plantation out of sheer curiosity, to see where the vegetables and fruits came from, how they were grown and processed.

Gonny must have recognized in me a kind of diamond in the rough, because in those days I had a rough appearance. That's almost impossible to imagine now. She herself was elegance personified, like a blonde Audrey Hepburn. She persuaded me to take up my education again. So I started to study law.

Later I came to work as a "contract and purchasing advisor" at the largest food company of the day with its headquarters in Rotterdam. I noticed that I often got fascinated by practical matters, such as ingredients and production processes. These ultimately interested me more than the legal and financial aspects. So two years later I became a raw materials purchaser. And later still, I became a purchasing consultant, a kind of trouble-shooter in the purchasing department, but even then only for raw materials, not semi-finished products. Colleagues sometimes called me 'Anton Smelt, de inkoopheld' (the purchasing hero).

It also meant that over the years I started traveling more and more. Sometimes Gonny would join me on my travels, often she couldn't, and sometimes she didn't want to. In some countries, traveling and staying overnight was not comfortable.

(Half a page has been torn out of the notebook here).

We were completely happy and then came colon cancer, chemotherapy, and later immunotherapy. A long battle that she eventually lost.

I probably feel the need to write this diary also because Gonny is no longer here. When she joined me on my travels we shared our impressions. If she didn't join me, I reported to her later in detail. She always enjoyed that. I treasured my memories because I knew I would tell her about them later. Now I am alone and I just write down what I experience and what I find remarkable.

June 6, 1978

I finally saw agoutis! Suddenly, early in the morning, a few were walking at the edge of the forest, on the grassy field. I think there were six of them. From the looks of it, they were searching for seeds and nuts. Last night there was a strong wind and I think all sorts of things fell from the trees onto the grass.
They look like large squirrels, but without the feathery tail. They are about the size of a cat or rabbit. I estimate their weight at 6 to 9 pounds. When they run on their slender legs, with intermittent jumps and bounds, they look like little antelopes with a fat posterior. Their coat is brown, shiny and smooth. *)

*) Post Scriptum: "It is greasy and has short brown and black hairs".

Much of the time they sit upright, looking around or holding something in their front feet. Besides seeds, I think they eat larvae or insects. I see them rooting among the blades of grass. Constantly foraging but also incessantly on their guard in an open field like this. Animals with eyes on either side of the head are prey for larger animals, such as, in this area, jaguars or ocelots.

Such fascinating animals! They make short squeaky and grunting sounds, like large guinea pigs. In rivalry among themselves, they will briefly bristle the hairs on the back of their bodies, making them appear larger. An extraordinary sight. They look like you could keep them as pets, like rabbits. But of course they are wild and apparently have extremely powerful jaws, against which perhaps no cage will be strong enough. Let alone your furniture.

June 7, 1978

So my earlier assumption is not correct. The agoutis are too small for Brazil nuts to pass through their bodies whole. I looked at the agouti's droppings and they are clearly narrower than a Brazil nut. That means they are crunching the nuts into small pieces, and so a new tree can never develop from that.

So, it is nice to know that the agouti can open the big fruit, take out the nuts and shell them, but there still won't be any new trees that way. Something else must be going on. Is there another animal that can open the hard fruit? A larger animal? Is there some other reason for going to all that trouble in order to open the rock-hard fruit other than for food?

Chico explained that very occasionally peccaries (little wild boars) or monkeys find and eat the loose Brazil nuts, but that they, too, bite the nuts to pieces.

I find it hard to accept that precisely with regard to the largest tree in the jungle, the tree that may outlive all other trees, the tree that is an important source of income for the local population, it is unknown how new ones emerge. Through what process, and by which steps?

June 21, 1978

It is clear that some villagers have to get used to my presence. Not everyone is convinced of my good intentions and some may see me as a rich tourist from whom there is something to be gained. They call me "el gringo", the stranger, which by the way has a neutral rather than a negative meaning here.

Yesterday some stuff disappeared from my home. Nothing valuable. I suspect it was stolen or borrowed. Maybe partly out of curiosity.

In a way, I can understand it. It is a tribal society here, where everyone owns about the same amount and many possessions are shared, either by the whole village or by one or several families. The ownership of unique personal possessions is associated with the role or task a person has in the village, which in turn tends to come with responsibilities.

I don't want to be romantic about it. There is undoubtedly greed and jealousy here, too, but cold-hearted theft usually does not make much sense when there's little difference between individual interests and tribal interests.

I've been in Puerto Maldonado briefly this morning to send a telex to my company, indicating that I will be staying longer. My assignment will be extended. I will make sure my interim reports are finished on time. With a borrowed typewriter and the telex- and fax-machines from the companies in town, that shouldn't be a problem.

Upon my return to the village, I met Nina. I immediately understood why she is called the jewel of the village. What a presence! She is bright and makes a very pleasant impression, has beautiful dark eyes and an enchanting broad smile. She speaks English, in addition to Spanish and Guarayo, of course. In Cusco she studied *Derecho,* Law, just like me. She feels at home in the village, but has clearly also seen more of the wider world.

June 24, 1978

Yesterday I spent a day with the nut harvesters. A farming family, father, mother, sons, cousins, all participate in the harvest, *el zafra.* They told me that each family manages a part

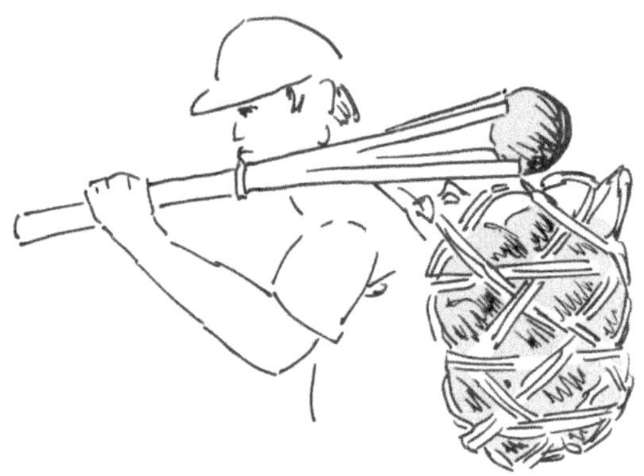

of the forest and collects the Brazil nuts there. They have a simple but extremely effective method for doing so.

On their backs they carry a large flexible basket with large meshes. The meshes are just slightly smaller than the smallest fruits.

The basket is put together in half an hour from materials taken from the jungle. On the side that sits against the back, they add some fresh leaves to prevent the clothes from getting dirty, because the fruits on the ground are often wet and muddy.

The tip of a straight branch of a tree that they call *parahuasca* is split into a four-toothed tool. With this *pallana* they pick the fruits from the ground. With a swoop of the arm, they then throw them over the shoulder into the basket one by one.

It's a handy tool that saves them from having to bend down all the time, but it is also a necessity: it is dangerous to reach for the ground with your hands every time. Snakes and scorpions, which are often well camouflaged, can hide in the damp leaves.

I asked if they ever climbed the tree to pick the fruit, but apparently that was a funny comment. No, they said, we take what the forest gives us. What's on the ground are the ripe, mature fruits. We only want those. They fall in the wet season. That means they lie on the damp ground for a long time, sometimes for months, before they are collected - which also accounts for the mold. If there are still many fruits left on the trees, they might come back two weeks later.

When everyone has a full basket, they meet at a certain spot in the forest. There the baskets are tipped over, creating a pile of more than one hundred and fifty, maybe two hundred fruits. Then the chopping begins.

I am struck by how moist the fruits are on the inside as well.
Of course, the chopping may also damage some of the nuts, or even get them chopped in half. Those end up as third choice, to be turned into flour or oil.
All loose nuts go into burlap sacks. The sacks are carried back on the backs of the gatherers to a clearing near the village.

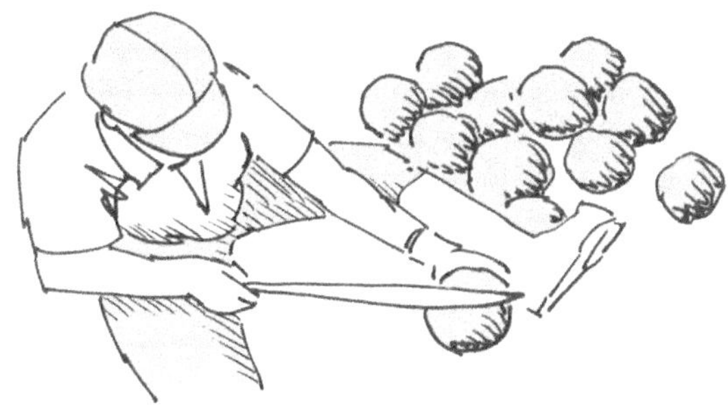

There is a *payol,* a type of shed consisting of a large shallow wooden trough with a mesh wire bottom and a sliding pointed roof. The nuts are washed and dried in the scorching sun. Eventually they go back into sacks and onto the boat to the big city.

The empty fruits are left behind in the forest. One of the gatherers explained that they have a special purpose there. During heavy rainfall, water collects in the open fruits. Various animals such as insects and frogs then live in them. Sometimes temporarily, sometimes their entire lives. They are small ponds in which they eat, sleep, mate, lay eggs.
I immediately feel the urge to turn over all the empty fruits lying on the ground so that their openings are facing up. Of course the gatherers thought that was very funny.

The villagers assigned me a patch of jungle for an experiment. It is located on higher ground, in an area where many animals come. It's about a half-hour's walk from Iyacu, depending on how much vegetation there is and how moist the ground is.

In the middle stands a beautiful Brazil nut tree. It is a young tree of about twenty years, which has just begun to produce fruits and therefore is not yet of much value to the family that gather the nuts in this area. Indeed, there were some fruits lying around the tree that were not very large.

In my mind, I call the piece of land "my little garden".

A compass is useless here because of the iron in some of the tree trunks. I find my orientation from the path that leads to this patch of land, pretending it is the south (in reality it is north-west). I give the trees names of cities I know. I call the Brazil nut tree Utrecht, and the surrounding trees I have given other place names, corresponding to their position. Den Helder and Groningen, for example, are respectively to the left and to the right, behind Utrecht.

I don't know exactly what I am going to do yet. I'm thinking about having a camera sent over from Holland and attaching it to one of the trees. With a wire attached to the shutter release, so that a picture is taken when an animal touches it.

Yesterday we spent all day trekking through the forest. Chico had said: I will show you the jungle sometime.

We slipped into a path behind his house and soon we were deep in the forest. There was no direct sunlight there. We kept to the tracks, but they were sometimes so narrow that we both needed a machete. Chico checked the machetes and handed me the blunter one, for the newly sharpened ones are as deadly as a samurai sword. One wrong move and your companion has to go to the hospital.

He explained that in this area many tracks are used for harvesting the Brazil nuts. These are maintained throughout the year, which guarantees that they do not become overgrown.

It was fascinating. At any given spot in the forest you are surrounded by at least twenty different trees and as many other plant species. The diversity is enormous. The same goes for the fauna; if you catch two butterflies in one day, chances are zero that they are of the same species. The same goes for the birds and snakes you see. And if you go out at night, you will see completely different animals.

Chico knew stories about dozens of plants and animals and was able to explain how to use them. For example for food, medicine, or making tools from them. He showed me a small tree with a slender trunk, which he called *yarumo* or *guarumo.* It seemed nothing special to me at first, but he slammed his fist against the trunk a few times, after which ants came crawling out of little holes everywhere. He explained that the ants live inside the tree; their entire ant colony is inside the trunk and the roots of the tree without harming it. The aggressive ants, in turn, keep fungi, caterpillars and other insects away. The ants even attack climbing plants and young plants that pop up in its vicinity.

By contrast, the birds and sloths that are responsible for spreading the seeds of the tree are left alone by the ants. The tree, which grows on low-nutrient soil, also extracts some of its food from the ants' droppings.

The tree rewards the ants by providing them with shelter and by producing some kind of nectar. Thus, both benefit.

Chico said, "Every guarumo lives with ants in it. If the ants were to leave, the tree would probably die."

There were many other plants of which Chico knew the particulars. One plant could be used to brew from against aching joints, another to pick edible maggots from, and another to extract red dye from, and so on. Each plant was like a closed book that Chico opened. The jungle as a giant library.

September 14, 1978

After many weeks, the crate with the camera finally arrived. I had given detailed instructions to my cousin in Holland and he had tried out the whole setup before sending the entire thing as fragile sea freight.

The camera will be placed on the periphery of "my little garden", directly opposite to the Brazil nut tree "Utrecht". Having mounted the camera against a tree trunk, I am not able to look through the viewfinder, but that is not a problem.

Through a tiny pulley, a long wire runs to the shutter release, within view of the lens, with a slack arc above the ground. When something touches the wire, a picture is taken.

I wrap the camera in burlap bags filled with rice, otherwise this kind of camera will give out too quickly in this humid climate. I hope the rice absorbs the moisture. I cover everything with a camouflage net. I don't know if this is necessary, but it does look professional.

So far, I have gone to check every other day. The camera has a counter that shows if a picture has been taken. This happens almost every day, which means it is pretty busy around that tree. Maybe I should check more often. I hope it's not peccaries all the time. Those animals sometimes have fixed routes that they follow with their squadron (their group) every day. That would be a shame. One time a branch had fallen on the wire, which will result in a photo of little interest.

September 18, 1978

I was briefly in Puerto Maldonado again to consult with the people of Planeta Peru. From the beginning, they were not enthusiastic about spraying with a fungicide. If that is done on a large scale, some of the poison will end up in the river, and the fungicide will then of course kill many more organisms, plants, algae, mosses.

Three alternatives were examined.
- Intensive washing tends to have the opposite effect.
- Heating in large drums to more than 160 °F. This is already being done and does not appear to help sufficiently against mold.
- Irradiating all nuts with ultraviolet light is complicated and very high-maintenance.

I consulted with Nina, and it is quite clear that the villagers reject the use of poison. Having the nuts shelled close to the source has several advantages. It also provides additional employment. In fact, it involves so much work that I wonder if enough people can be made available during those few months a year.
It will involve quite a logistical reorganization. The nuts are currently stockpiled in a number of cities such as Puerto Maldonado. There will have to be central workshops for shelling the nuts. That makes more sense than shelling the nuts in the countless small villages. The initial washing and drying will still be done in the jungle, on the payols. But we can learn a lot from how it is currently done in Spain.
The fungus mainly develops after the harvest due to humid storage of unshelled nuts. Rapid processing will therefore be important. It will reduce the chance of exposing local people to the carcinogenic mold to nil.

October 22, 1978

The photos are in! I had four films of 24 pictures developed and immediately printed in Puerto Maldonado. I assured the owner of Inkafarma (a photo store cum drugstore, perfumery and pharmacy) that the photos were important and unique. But it all went fine, and I got them back in a nice cardboard box.

Nina immediately noticed that the photos had come to the village by taxi boat, so we looked at them together.
In many photos nothing can be seen, and it is unclear what touched the wire.
Two photos show a jaguar or ocelot. Put more accurately, one shows a tail and the other one is a blurred photo of the coat, with its beautiful markings up close.
Some of the photos show peccaries, the little wild boars that roam the jungle in groups, searching for anything edible. I hadn't noticed it, but Nina points out to me that a little bird can be seen in the background. It is a rare ground cuckoo that follows the peccaries and picks up the scraps they leave behind. Small seeds and berries, as well as insect larvae exposed in the upturned soil.

The peccaries travel along fixed routes and almost every day that little bird is there. So the natives call it the "peccary bird". Each squadron (group of boars) has its own bird. Sometimes this bird also follows groups of monkeys and eats the fallen fruit. It seems to be an intelligent little bird.

Nina's focus was clearly on the photos, but I still sensed something. She sat against me and we shared our enthusiasm about the photos. I could easily have misinterpreted the fact that she was sitting so close to me. Most people here keep little distance, touching you briefly when they greet you, want your attention, or get emotional.

That reminds me of something else: they no longer call me *el gringo.* Recently I have become *señor Antón,* with the emphasis on the second syllable.

Of course, it was all about the agoutis. And they are in the pictures as well, and I can see that they scurry off with large open fruits as well as single seeds. These are still images, of course, but it seems as if each agouti runs off with the seeds almost immediately and does not eat them on the spot. This is different from what I had seen earlier on the grassy field, where they ate seeds quietly, sitting upright. I don't see that anywhere in these photos. What causes this difference?

October 24, 1978

Why hadn't I thought of this before!!

There are so many nuts in this fruit that the agouti always has some left. It's almost as if the tree is making sure that there are more nuts in it than an agouti can eat right away.

I had seen a lot of opened fruits, of course, but I didn't realize it until I was absent-mindedly playing with nuts in an opened fruit I had in my home and I intuitively started counting them. Immediately I walked into the village to ask some questions to a random villager. A large fruit can contain up to 24 nuts. They are arranged more or less like segments in a tangerine, but where a citrus fruit contains one whorl of segments, so to speak, the nuts of a Brazil-nut fruit are arranged in two or even three irregularly shaped whorls stacked onto each other.

But what does the agouti do with them? Does it bury the leftover nuts? Does it make stockpiles, like a squirrel? In the photos I can see that they open the fruit and make off with the nuts or with the open fruit, but what happens next, down the road, is still a mystery to me. How can I find out?

November 8, 1978

Nina and I were in Puerto Maldonado yesterday. We had a final discussion about the plans of organizing the shelling of the nuts there. Everyone is excited and confident.

In theory, it is quite simple. All the processes that now take place in Spain will be transferred to Peru. The rest of the chain remains unchanged.
One of the purchasing agents outlined the current process on a large roll of paper. That is, a process based on exporting the nuts in their shells. A vertical blue line separates the work done in Peru from the work done in Spain. After the discussion, I take a

marker and draw a new line, further to the right. And I cross out the word "Spain". Completely unexpectedly, some of the people present begin to applaud. It's as if I have cut a ribbon.

This will be a big deal between our company, Planeta Peru in Puerto Maldonado, and the Spanish companies. The complete inventory of the Spanish companies will be bought up, for the most part, be moved to Puerto Maldonado and two other cities. This should happen in the next four months, during the rainy season, so everything will be ready for the harvest that begins next May.
For this forced reorganization we will apply for a subsidy from the EEC, because the contracts with the Spanish companies will have to be bought off. Next, we will have to find as many workers as possible among the people in the province who have other sources of income outside the harvesting season of Brazil nuts.

November 9, 1978

This morning I went to look at the river and stayed on the small jetty for a while. The rainy season has begun and the river is clearly much higher and still rising. The water seems even less transparent than usual. Leaves, a tree stump, or branches float by continuously. Also planks and objects made of brightly colored plastic materials. Sometimes a whole tree.
The sound of the jungle orchestra has also changed. Many more frogs can be heard. Even during daytime.

I'm trying to picture all the rivers in the Amazon, the branches of the Amazon river, and their sub-branches. They all empty into the ocean. Each hour they transport countless tons of washed-up soil, full of organic matter and nutrients. A Dutch marine biologist in Indonesia once told me that this material from the rain forests is probably an important food source for the plankton in the oceans. The plankton that produces one-third of the world's oxygen.

I imagine how centuries ago the Inca culture flourished here with their mighty cities in the jungle. They must have had a rain god who caused the rainy season with an annual torrent of tears. I'll have to ask someone about that.

November 14, 1978

I delivered my final report. And returned the borrowed typewriter. The stack of typed sheets, together with handwritten notes, were faxed to the Netherlands. After I had received a confirmation of receipt for this, I also sent everything by registered and insured mail. If my advice is taken, the implementation, that whole financial and logistical operation, will largely take place without any involvement from me.

Now that the villagers are going to shell the nuts by themselves, they will need to do the selection as well. The initial selection is based on buoyancy. Empty shells that contain no nut at all (called *chias*) are considerably lighter than full ones. After that, the nuts are heated in a tumble drier (between 160 and 210 °F). This causes them to dry out a little on the inside and loosen from the shell. Depending on the humidity, this can take up to two days.

The nuts are shelled by means of small, manually operated pressing machines. It's fascinating to see how skillful people are with these and how many nuts are cracked in a short time.
Then they are divided into three categories. Perfect nuts are first choice. Second choice means slightly damaged or slightly different in shape or color. These end up in chocolate or in nut mixes, for example. Very small and damaged nuts will be third choice. These are used for the production of flour and oil.

Removing the shells from the nuts reduces their surface area, but it also halves their total volume. This makes storage under good climatic conditions easier. And, in turn, this helps to prevent the growth of mold.

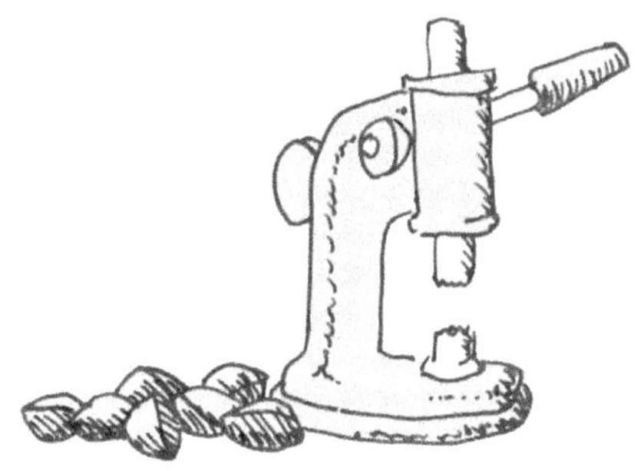

The harbingers of the rainy season have arrived. Planks that are covering some of the village's most-trodden paths because of the soggy ground are getting inspected, and are straightened or replaced if necessary. Structures are strengthened and trenches are cleaned and dug deeper.

In the field, the fertile ashes from burned organic waste are scattered. These ashes have been accumulated for a year and can now be absorbed deep into the soil with the rain.

The torrential rains are preceded by brief showers, which regularly take me by surprise. As a *gringo* I am not very good at forecasting the changes in the weather, so the villagers sometimes see me running across the field soaking wet.

1979

It looks like the rainy season is over. Three dry days in a row, they say here. The torrential rains limit a great many activities, but part of nature is actually flourishing. Plants are developing fruits, and for some animals it is mating time.

Today, after months, I visited Puerto Maldonado again to do some shopping. It usually suffices to give a shopping list to somebody from the village, but this time it would require a little more effort and knowledge.
I quickly found the blue fabric at the market. The fabric was sold by the linear meter. I needed much less. I paid for one meter and then asked the market lady for a much smaller piece. *Gringo loco* she must have thought.

For the fishing line and screws, I had to search a little longer, but I finally found both in a department store. I cut the fishing line into pieces of about two feet long. To one end I will fasten a piece of blue fabric of about 5-by-5 inches (never mind having no ruler here). To the other end a screw will be fastened that fits in the germination aperture of a Brazil nut.

I place twelve nuts in a row near my tree "Utrecht". The fishing lines point one way, and I cover the little flags with a few leaves so they don't stand out too much. I don't think that is necessary, but you never know. There might be a bird in the forest that finds the blue patches attractive. I expect the agouti's instincts

to be so strong that the fishing line and the little flag make no difference.

The blue flags contrast well with all the colors of the jungle. That way, no matter what happens to them, I hope to be able to retrieve the nuts without problem later on. I got that idea because, when I was a ship's cook, we used blue Band Aids in the galley. The color blue was chosen to prevent any of them from getting into the food unnoticed.

May 13, 1979

Today Chico and I went deep into the jungle. We left early. I thought maybe at some point we would get near the freeway. It is located somewhere parallel to the river, but at a few miles' distance away from it. I didn't see or hear the road. We did hear chain saws every now and then in the distance. Never a pleasant sound in the jungle, even if it sounds very soft and far away. It is as irritating as these lanky youngsters with their mopeds. In any case, it does not bode well.

Chico listens to how long the periods of sawing and intermittent pauses last. I hear him swear. He thinks they are poachers looking for nests of young parrots. These people operate in a heavy-handed way. They don't just plunder nests, they actually cut down the trees.

Parrots, he says, are picky when it comes to the tree cavities they nest in, and those cavities are reused every breeding season. Year-on-year there are not enough suitable places for couples that want to hatch their eggs. Nesting couples even fight among themselves to get one. So when such trees are cut down, in order to plunder a nest one time, it is an instant disaster for future generations. This way there will be fewer nests and consequently fewer young parrots.

There are still lots of parrots, Chico says, so it seems nothing is wrong, but if you look closely they are all older birds. There is not much new young stock. so because of the poaching and other threats, the population will be a lot smaller in 20 or 30 years' time.

May 22, 1979

I waited a few days before describing my experiment with the little flags, because the first attempt had failed. Probably some peccaries had dropped by and made quite a mess of "my little garden". It was chaos. I recovered only a few of my flags and none of the nuts.

Chico explained that the peccaries roam about early in the day.

Agoutis are active much later, until dusk sets in. So a few days later I distributed the nuts again. In the early afternoon, and the next day I went out early to have a look. I scoured the ground for specks of blue on the brown-green soil. I walked around my tree "Utrecht" in ever increasing circles.

Out of twelve flagged nuts, the score is:
- 2 were still more or less in their original places
- 4 nuts I found buried in the ground, with their little flags visible above the surface
- 1 was not buried and was found far away from the tree
- 1 flag I retrieved without a nut
- 4 I did not retrieve at all

By the way, the nuts are often buried in small stashes of 3 to 6. So it also happens that a nut with a flag is lying among other nuts without a flag.

Out of the two nuts that had not been moved, one was empty. An empty shell, that happens sometimes. It was a "blank" that I hadn't noticed. Could the agoutis have sensed it, that saving that nut made no sense? I could look into that but don't know if I'm going to.

I left everything as I found it. Close to each buried nut, I marked a tree to make them even easier to find. I also gave each flag a number, using a marker and I drew a map for myself with the position of the nuts and their numbers on it. This may all sound very scientific, but I am just winging it. Moreover, I am limited by the materials available here. Fortunately, I do have plenty of time to think about such an experiment and prepare it properly.

Anyway, so the agouti buries the remaining nuts! It amazes me that the relocated nuts are taken so far from the tree. A few hundred yards. The five nuts with flags that I did not recover may have been buried even further from the tree.

May 24, 1979

I hadn't had a very clear reason for it, but numbering the flags was a good decision. The next day I found that, out of 4 buried nuts, 3 had disappeared. Of these, I retrieved 2, which had been buried in a new location. One I found almost half a mile away from the original tree! Seriously, the same or some other agoutis dig up the nuts and hide them somewhere else. Whether coincidentally or intentionally, they take them even further away from the tree. If this is done by other agoutis, it is a kind of theft.

I realize that if an agouti buries a small stash of nuts, of course it will still eat them later. So that doesn't result in a new tree either. Only if the little critter forgets about a stash, is unable to find it again, or if an agouti dies, for instance in the jaws of an ocelot, will the stash remain in place. Those chances are not very great if you consider that they apparently know how to find each other's stashes effortlessly. So those buried nuts are actually there for all the agoutis in the area.

It is almost funny: if the agouti is solely responsible for distributing the nuts, then this is an exclusive partnership. The trees, and perhaps even the agoutis, survive only if individual agoutis die or forget about their stashes.

Simply put: *It only works out well if something goes wrong.*

June 1979

Nina thinks the chainsaws have to do with illegal land acquisition by big landowners. These people are constantly destroying parts of the jungle and turning it into farmland. It often involves shady deals, nepotism and forged documents. Plots of land that have been managed and used by a certain village or tribe for centuries suddenly turn out to have been sold to someone at some point. And it's ostensibly been done in a completely legal way.

Nina talks about it calmly, but I can tell she's getting agitated, for her cheeks are turning red.

From the main road, farmers penetrate ever further into the jungle with a combination of cutting, sawing and burning. The forest will then turn into pasture for cattle, or it will become a place where corn or soy is grown. This is the biggest threat to the jungle. Each minute, a piece of jungle the size of four soccer fields disappears. Forever.

In much of the Peruvian jungle, the Brazil nut tree is being protected, but the rest of the forest is not. And when everything is cut down and turned into farmland with some stray Brazil-nut trees here and there, the epiphytes and orchid bees won't come. That means the trees eventually become locally extinct. So this protection is just a crock.

Yesterday I took a short trip through the forest with Chico. He explained that dozens of organisms live in each tree: plants and animals, birds, fungi, you name it. A whole world unto itself. Each tree species has a unique composition of insects that live on it. Some of those insects are found only on that one species. And there is also a difference between the insects that live in the lower part of the tree, in the middle, and at the very top.

When saplings begin to grow near an existing tree, they are immediately eaten by the insects that live on the lower part of the tree trunk. Therefore, the survival of the species requires that the seeds of the tree be moved to a place further away. Also, the soil there is probably richer in the necessary nutrients than close to a large tree of the same species.

The agouti spreads the seeds for the Brazil nut tree. What drives the agouti to bury the nuts so far from the tree? Is it purely a matter of finding a suitable spot, or is there more to it?
Of course, for the survival of the tree species, it only matters where the forgotten seeds are buried. The seeds that are dug up later and get eaten will never become a tree.

My photos are only a snapshot in time, but I have the impression that the agoutis never linger around near the tree for long, and quickly scurry off with their stashes. But why? Is it because of competition from other agoutis?

June 1979

The survival of the tree requires that the nuts be buried. That way they will be safe from hungry insects and mammals such as monkeys and peccaries. So the tree needs help with that.

Today I suddenly realize that each tree species designs its seeds, nuts or fruits in such a sophisticated way that their shape and appearance provide sufficient protection from pests and, at the same time, are optimal for the method of distribution.

If seeds are scattered by the wind, they will be light and will have to fall on nutritious soil. On the other hand, large seeds contain their own supply of energy. These need to protect themselves from large and small animals that regard them as food. Other trees form fruits around the seeds, which attract animals (monkeys, birds) and thus guarantee the distribution of the seeds.

The color of blackberries, the thickness of the apple skin, the seeds of the dandelion, the hollow coconut, the number of Brazil nuts in a fruit, everything. Everything has a reason. Each plant species, as it were, "designs" its seeds so that they are optimally protected and optimally distributed. The routes the seeds follow, all the help they receive, and all the dangers they encounter in the meantime, it all determines what they look like. And then there is timing. At what time of year is a fruit ripe, when does it fall off the tree, when are chestnuts released from their spiny husk, etc.

July 1979

Every now and then some news from Europe gets through to the village. Usually after someone has been to the big city or when there is some news on the radio. I have never seen a Dutch newspaper here, but I did see an English or Spanish one. I read something about the oil crisis and high unemployment, Lubbers in the Netherlands, Thatcher in England.
Is that what I want to return to? Iyacu and its surroundings seem so idyllic in comparison, despite the harsh reality, despite all the things that seem to be missing here, despite the climate.

I have lived here for a year and two months now. The fact that not everything is always available here is something I have come to see as an asset. The seasons make their influence felt. That means that sometimes I long for a fruit or vegetable that is not available right then. Or that I have been able to get something from the market for weeks that is suddenly no longer there. "Back again in eight months" is the response I then get with a friendly smile. It makes me appreciate it even more when a product is available again later on.

I am thinking about letting my company know that I'm resigning. Or that I will retire early and stay here for the time being. The things that need to be done here and my role in them seem much more appealing than going back to the Netherlands and waiting for the next job, somewhere else in the world.

July 1979

I had wanted to do this much earlier, but now I have finally started to plant some nuts myself. Villagers tell me that long ago they had also planted nuts in the jungle, hoping that eventually more Brazil nut trees would grow there, but it has never produced a new tree.

I use the drawers from Padre Luís' desk and some soil I got from the jungle. To be able to also bury some of the nuts extra deep, I managed to get hold of a large oil drum. It is all standing next to my house, where there is a lot of sunlight, especially in the afternoon. Of course, I also planted nuts in the jungle. In "my little garden" I demarcated a rectangular parcel of land and buried nuts there at three different depths.

July 24, 1979

The news came over the radio this morning. Like a bombshell: The chainsaws we heard earlier are not from poachers but from the activities of surveyors. The government in Cusco intends to build a dam downstream with a hydroelectric power station to generate electricity, so-called "white coal". A joint venture of Energía Peru and a Brazilian energy company.

This would mean that a huge area will be flooded. The area here has little difference in elevation. The dam will make the water rise by over thirty yards. That may not seem much for a dam, but it will result in a lake that covers a huge area, including more than ten villages. It is estimated that more than two thousand people will then have to move. This is the land they live on, where they know every path and every plant. This is the area where they not only live, this is their farmland, their refrigerator and medicine cabinet, where they have buried their ancestors, this is their culture.

As a result, the indigenous population is not only losing its territory, but actually its entire way of life. This also includes the parts of the jungle that have been allocated to families for the harvest of Brazil nuts. The nuts are an important source of income, especially in the months after the wet season when few other crops can be harvested.

August 7, 1979

I had started storing a few nuts because I wanted to see how long a nut would stay viable. And whether a nut could still take root after, say, two or three years. But then Nina came up with a fantastic idea.

In this region, when a child is born, a present is given in the form of a a ball-shaped rattle made from twigs and pieces of deer skin. They are quite large and contain unshelled Brazil nuts. In the village there is a boy who is almost three years old and a girl who is over five.

With much deliberation and charm, Nina asks for the nuts and replaces them with new ones. Fortunately, there is no superstition to prevent that.

Now I have seven nuts of over five years old and as many nuts of nearly three years old that I can plant to see if they will germinate and come alive. I do realize that these nuts have not been buried deep in the ground all this time.

August 11, 1979

I don't get to hear everything that goes on in the village. That's not a bad thing, but I do notice it. With some events, the villagers think it is none of my business, that I won't understand it, or that I won't find it interesting.

Yesterday there was a hearing in the big city. I didn't know anything about it. There were representatives of the residents of the area, people from the government, and people from the companies that are going to build the dam. The villagers had brought ritual spears. There were also guards in uniform. I heard that things got heated, but fortunately there were no serious incidents.

August 14, 1979

I resigned. Ha! I decided to stay here permanently. Yesterday I went into town to arrange everything by telex and fax (because of the signatures).

It had been on my mind for some time. Sure, I do feel a responsibility toward my company, but a lot has changed there. Some product groups have been divested, while there was expansion in the States. People are being laid off, but at the same time young colleagues are coming in. They have just completed their education and handle many things differently.

When I imagine the rest of my life here, in the jungle, by the river, it just feels comfortable. Despite the mosquitoes, spiders, ants, snakes, and the sporadic assault on my intestines. Financially, it shouldn't be a problem. With the sale of the house and a farewell present from the company.

Nina came and sat with me on the porch today. She didn't say much, and she didn't need to. We looked across the grassy field, how every now and then someone walked from one house to another. And we heard the jungle orchestra in the background.

She brought a beverage made from the fruit of the lucumo. There are fruits growing here that no one in Europe has ever heard of, and sometimes they make juices from them. Aguaymanto, camucamu, jaboticaba, chirimoya. I have a hard time remembering the names. All the names here seem composed of a limited alphabet.

In the big city, many places serve *chicha morada,* a refreshing drink made of black corn with other fruits, cinnamon and cloves. Half in jest, we raised our glasses and of course I looked her in the eye. Outside in the sunlight, Nina's eyes glowed like gems, but in the shadow of the porch, her irises were as black as her pupils. What is this? Am I falling in love again? At my age?

The drink tasted fresh, not too sweet, and with a complex flavor, citrus and caramel.

September 7, 1979

This past week the first plants have come up. The nuts I planted in the desk drawers and the oil drum have sprouted, not all of them, but most of them have. The ones in the desk drawers are not doing great. They seem to grow slower than the ones in the oil drum; I suspect because there is not enough room for the roots to grow downward.

Young plants all look alike. So to make sure it's not another plant whose seed has been brought in with the soil, I dug a few out. But they are all Brazil nuts.

It is such an everyday occurrence and yet so special; the young plant growing up from the nut and the root going exactly the other way. The young plant consumes the nut as it were; it's the plant's food supply for the first few days or weeks in order to develop its roots and its first green leaves. Then more leaves appear and they convert sunlight to the energy needed to continue growing.

But the nuts I buried in my little garden in the forest are not taking root. I dug a few out again, disturbed them in their sleep. Not even the beginnings of a root or plant can be seen.
At first I thought maybe the agouti is doing something to the nuts to prevent them from taking root. Does it bite something off? Does it have enzymes in its saliva to cover the nut with so that the roots don't develop? But the nuts I planted in the forest were never touched by an agouti.
I am puzzled. Why do they grow in the containers next to my house, but not in the jungle where they belong? When does a new tree develop in nature? Am I completely wrong? Does it have nothing to do with the agoutis and is there some other animal that distributes the nuts?

September 22, 1979

In Puerto Maldonado, I gave a presentation on the economic importance of the area that will be flooded if construction of the dam goes ahead. About the importance of the Brazil nuts as a source of income for hundreds of families outside the season when other crops are harvested.

It was not a huge success. It was unclear who were present; government, Energía Peru, construction companies. As a result, I found it difficult to hit the right note.
I switched too much between the importance of the Brazil nut harvest, of the preservation of the jungle and the importance of the culture of the local people. Moreover, my Spanish is limited and also differs from the variety spoken here. My Spanish tends to sound more informal, which doesn't help me come across in a professional way.
Fortunately, I did have images and numbers on a flip chart, to which Nina had added some Spanish and Guarayo words.

There were moments when some of the audience nodded in agreement, while others showed that they clearly disagreed. It was also striking that some people knew nothing at all about the harvesting of Brazil nuts and their economic importance to the population of this large area. At the very least, I brought some contradictory views into the open. Let's hope that's progress.

September 23, 1979

I helped with the work in preparation for the rainy season. We repaired structures, straightened or replaced the planks covering the tracks, deepened the ditches, etc. We are ready.

1980

The rainy season is mostly over and we are busy cleaning everything up again. When the river overflows its banks, the water does not reach the village and the land beyond, but due to the heavy rain, the paths are still covered with leaves, branches, and sometimes whole tree trunks. By the looks of it, the cleanup is mostly done by men and boys, with one experienced man leading the way. The small children and mothers stay in the village and the most they do is clean up the periphery of the village, like removing branches from the grassy field.

The ground is incredibly soft and still wet from all the rain. Walking is tiresome. Even where there are no puddles, with each step my feet sink maybe six inches into the soil, which consists of mud and plant material. It is like our autumn: all the dead material has fallen off the trees due to the rain and landed on the ground.

My necklace with the locket had come off, but fortunately I noticed it hanging at the bottom of my shirt just in time. I have to be careful with it. The clasp is bent and I don't think I can get it fixed here in the jungle.

I finally understand why the agouti takes the nuts so far from the tree in order to bury them!

We had spent all week clearing the paths of branches and other material. While doing the cleaning up, the villagers try to estimate the quantity of Brazil nuts. If there are many, they have to get relatives from other villages to help with the harvest. If there are few, they can do it themselves.

After the last day of cleaning up, I sit on my porch in the evening. It is warm and I am enjoying a beer for the first time in months. On the edge of the porch I have placed kerosene lamps. Someone had brought me the fuel from the big city earlier. I stare at the insects circling the lanterns. Some burn and drop onto the planks of the porch. I doze off.
At a certain moment I see a gecko approaching from the other corner of the porch. Moving slowly from the darkness into the light. Attracted not by the kerosene lamps, but by the buzzing and fluttering insects. With quick movements, the reptile snaps at the insects that land on the planks.

It still takes at least another 15 minutes before I see it, understand the metaphor unfolding before my eyes. The kerosene lamp is the tree, the light is the nuts. The flies are the agoutis and the gecko is an actual predator. Of course the agoutis make off with the nuts! If they linger around the tree every time, predators will visit the tree more and more frequently; felines, but also snakes. So in order not to fall prey to any of these predators they make off with the nuts. And then they eat and bury the nuts at a considerable distance from the tree.

Agoutis, of course, are unaware of the benefit to the Brazil nut tree, nor of the role they play in spreading the seeds. It is a behavior that has evolved over countless centuries.

June 12, 1980

Yesterday there was some news on the radio from a village further down the river, near the freeway. There had been a clash between the local population and a caravan of vehicles involved in the construction of the dam. There was one death on the side of the villagers. In a number of villages roadblocks had been set up. The villagers carried spears, but these are part of their traditional attire rather than real weapons.

They could do little against the bulldozers and trucks. And then the construction companies also deployed their gang of goons. I don't know what else to call them. They wear nondescript uniforms. Sometimes it is completely unclear whether they are from the police or the military, whether they are acting on behalf of the government or are making some extra money on the side. Then there are different types of police. They typically include the county and local police, who, when it comes to corruption, sometimes have conflicting interests and compete with each other as if they were part of the mafia. The gang of goons at the construction site may also consist of mercenaries, and they may not even be Peruvians.

In the end, the villagers were no match for the enormous caravan of vehicles and it was able to move on even before the ambulance had arrived.

Clearly, there is serious concern here in the region. The atmosphere has changed. A number of people from different villages have already been to the capital to submit a protest to the governor, but so far without result.

Today we got some other news. One of the neighboring villages was shot at from a helicopter. There are no casualties, just some property damage and one animal is dead, a dog or goat, I heard. The helicopter had "the colors of the jungle", they say. That could mean the military, or perhaps a helicopter discarded by the army. I have no idea.

Energía Peru and the companies that want to build the dam are known, but it remains unclear to what extent they receive support from the police or military and whether it is legal.

A feeling of insecurity is slowly getting me in its grip. I haven't had that here before. The jungle was strange and sometimes impenetrable in more ways than one, but not hostile. Neither were the people.

June 1980

Almost forgot to write something about the old nuts I planted in a container next to my house.

Out of the 7 nuts that are almost 3 years old, 4 have germinated. Out of the 7 nuts that are over 5 years old, only 1 has germinated. The five young plants are looking good. I am impressed. The nuts may spend years in some kind of hibernation, but even so they will germinate.

June 25, 1980

I spent the night with Nina.

Yesterday Puerto Maldonado celebrated the festival of San Juan, patron saint of the Amazon rivers. The Christian festival has merged with *Inti Raymi,* the traditional sun festival of the Incas. According to Nina, it is the most important festivity of the year. There was dancing, music, sports. All aspects of Peruvian jungle culture were celebrated, it seems. Many people wore folkloristic costumes, which made it extra attractive to watch the dancing. Once or twice I got to try to participate in a dance, but I was mostly watching and listening. And eating. On the street, free *juanes* were handed out; packages of rice with chicken and olives specially made for this day, wrapped in banana leaf and representing the severed head of John the Baptist.

I saw Nina in a group performing a traditional dance. The women were scantily clad and, swaying their hips, held a water pitcher on their heads. Later I saw her in a white folkloristic dress, which is a vestige from the time of Spanish rule I suspect. A lot of petticoats, like tutus, a red sash around her waist, and a round straw hat.

I marveled at how she seemed to feel at home everywhere; in the jungle, at the university, at this festival, and it reminded me of how her fellow villagers called her "the jewel of the village".

We returned home earlier than most of our fellow villagers. In the taxi boat on the way back, Nina asked what I had done all day and what I thought of it, but we were mostly silent. We were still glowing after a beautiful day.

Arriving at the village, Nina took my hand and walked with a little spring in her step. We didn't speak. It was as if we were silently sharing each other's thoughts. The village was deserted. Everyone was still at the festival in the big city. She told me that most of the villagers stayed up all night partying, were getting very drunk, and wouldn't be returning until the next morning.

Almost without my noticing it, we had arrived at Nina's house. At the porch steps, she suddenly turned around, kissed me full on the mouth, carefully lowered herself backwards on the steps, and pulled me over on top of her. I felt no hesitation. I felt how long I had longed for her, her lips, her arms, everything. I became eager, her folkloristic skirts were in the way. We went inside, and I stayed the night.

Today I watched a soccer game. Every now and then, in the afternoon, the children of the village are playing soccer on the grass between the houses. The bright colors of their T-shirts and shorts contrast with their dark skin, black hair and the green color of the grass. Sitting on my porch, I can watch it for a very long time without really following the game, without knowing who is scoring or what the score is. It reminds me of the colorful Calder-like mobile that used to hang from the ceiling in my study. I had once bought it as a construction kit in the museum store at the MoMA. On beautiful days, I would open the window just to get more movement from it.

Watching the children playing, a feeling of contentment comes over me, the idea that I no longer need anything and have everything of importance within reach. Nothing else matters.

As dusk set in, Nina joined me. She told me that her brother was coming to visit soon. She didn't say anything else, asked nothing, and watched the same spectacle. We were like a young couple at the cinema. It has been a long time since I have felt so happy, so complete.

July 3, 1980

I could have thought of it before, but it now occurred to me that, of course, all that shelling of nuts is going to create a huge pile of waste. I asked Nina what could be done with it. She suggested that in due course some of it could be used to fire the oven that heats the nuts before they are shelled. Perhaps it would be a good idea to take the shells back to the jungle and disperse them there, thus slowly letting them become part of the soil again. After all, that is where the shells also end up when the agoutis and other animals leave them behind.

Nina said they could also simply be thrown into the river. That may sound crude, but, as a matter of fact, it would be no problem at all. I have yet to enquire how the people in Spain solved this. Nina fantasized that they could also be made into unique jewelry, earrings, bracelets, pendants. Good for exports.

July 1980

Yesterday Tino, Nina's younger brother, visited us. Beforehand, she had told me that he works in a gold mine. I didn't query her about it because she had told me that it would take him two hours to get here on foot. That means the gold mine is in the Tambopata area and most likely illegal.

Tino brought some pork and together they prepared a stew from it. In addition, they made mashed potatoes and vegetables and some salad. Their parents were also there, of course. We sat outdoors in the grassy field, with half of Ninas' kitchen set up outside. The brightly colored plastic dishes and ditto utensils added to the festive spirit. There was a lot of chatter and laughter. I tried to follow it as best I could. By now I recognize a few

Guarayo words, but even so I still don't understand what is being said.

Nina told her brother about the cockroaches in Padre Luís' desk drawer. Tino replied in Guarayo. I didn't understand it, but there were a lot of 'k' sounds in it, and it sounded far from positive. He turned to me and told me that Padre Luís had been involved in many shadowy affairs and that he now probably held a missionary post in Tierra del Fuego, close to the South Pole.

After the meal, I made coffee. Tino then told me that the meat he had brought was from agoutis. He thought it was a big joke that he made me eat agouti because I was so concerned about the critters.

I played along and immediately ran to the back of the house and made noises like I was throwing up.

As I walked back, I saw that Nina looked worried. I gave her a wink. In truth, I had long known that agoutis were eaten and had wondered what it would taste like. It was indeed a bit like pork.

July 1980

Seen a harpy eagle! What a fantastic experience.

It is a large bird of prey, over 3 feet tall, named after the terrifying creatures of Greek mythology. It lives in the treetops; the dense canopy is actually the 'bottom' of its world. Up there it has its nest and hunts monkeys, sloths, and smaller birds. It never actually goes to the ground, only by accident or when there is very little prey to be found.

I thought I could see that it (I have no idea if it was a male or female) was struggling to move in the dense jungle, now that it had sunk through the canopy. Eventually it made its way up among the tree trunks, with audible beats of its huge wings, and found an exit. A patch of blue sky among the green vegetation. Thus it escaped back to the upper world.

That was yesterday. I had gone for a walk because many villagers had left for the big city to vote.

There were presidential elections, but, equally important, elections for the governor of this province. Much depends on it. The current governor supports the plans for the dam and is in favor of large farms. The left-wing opposition candidate is against the dam and champions the interests of indigenous people.

July 1980

I haven't written about this before, but I had sent for a *curandero*, a medicine man.

Nina said, "If you have so many questions you can't find answers to, then ask them in a different way", and she recommended a shamanic session with yagé *). I had heard of it and read about

) nowadays better known as ayahuasca.

it. It is mentioned in the accounts of the botanist Richard Spruce, so I was not entirely unfamiliar with it. Yet I needed time to get used to the idea of ever doing it myself. Nina assured me, that under the guidance of an experienced curandero, nothing could go wrong.

The preparations were extensive. Five days on a diet of unprocessed local food, no pork, no sugar, alcohol or coffee. In addition, several conversations with an elderly villager, with Nina as interpreter, to fine-tune my expectations. He asked at length what pains, frustrations or unprocessed emotions I had. I told about the mysteries of the Brazil nuts and, of course, about Gonny's passing. The old man said, "Maybe she will come to you, you will see her, maybe not at all."
Then, two days ago, it was time for the session. There would be two other participants. In the morning, a curandero had come over from a nearby village. While he was making preparations, I did not eat anything all day. About an hour before the ceremony, I and the other two were showered with flowers by women from the village, to facilitate contact with the jungle, they said. The children are sent inside and the dogs are muzzled against barking. Sudden noises are said to be very disturbing to those who participate in a yagé session.

We sit outside, on the huge porch of one of the villagers. Candles are everywhere, providing a soft diffused light. The curandero moves quietly as if he has done this hundreds of times before, but otherwise he looks no different from any other Peruvian: Sandals, jeans, a white shirt under a dark blue casual sweater. No poncho, no feather headdress, no facial paint. He does have a bottle of rum within easy reach, though.

It is slowly getting dark outside. The other two speak both Guarayo and English, so I can communicate indirectly with the curandero if necessary. I am not nervous, just curious about what will happen.

The ceremony begins when the medicine man blows smoke into my face to cleanse me, make me receptive to the yagé. One by one, we are handed a small bowl. The bowl is perfectly round and resembles half a Brazil nut fruit. The drink tastes bitter like a mixture of mud and plants, much like the soil of the jungle.

In a few sips, I empty the bowl. I continue to wait quietly. For the first half hour I notice nothing, except a bitter aftertaste like that of tobacco. I try to relax. I slump down a bit and listen to the singing of the curandero.

When I briefly close my eyes I see some geometric figures flash up. But those I also see sometimes when I rub my eyes.

I get a second bowl to drink and almost immediately have to throw up. My body starts getting heavier and I begin to sweat profusely. The curandero gestures that I should lie down. I stare at the ceiling, the roof of leaves just barely visible in the candle light. Then I close my eyes again.

The first thing I notice is hard to describe. It's a deep sense of contentment, the idea that I'm in my element and that everything is the way it is meant to be.

I feel my arms and legs slowly separate from my torso. At first I resist that idea, but the feeling is too strong. They drift away from me. I make a surprised sound and a moment later the candlelight around me is extinguished.

My hands and feet get detached, and then my toes and fingers slowly drift away from me. For a brief moment I think I am dying, but I feel no fear. My whole body breaks up into ever smaller parts, like a swarm of bees. Finally it bursts apart and each particle is absorbed by the jungle like smoke from a campfire rising through the branches. I now feel literally without a body and part of the forest. It is as if we are breathing simultaneously, as if the juices in the tree trunks are forming my bloodstream, the snakes becoming my fingers, the ocelot's paws becoming my feet. I experience all the animals and plants down to the smallest insects and worms, the whole forest alive and breathing.

Slowly I notice that the space between all these elements fills up with long transparent tubes that become increasingly bright and colorful. From tree to insect to bird to predator, countless little tubes swarm from the ground and around the trunks, tubes shoot through the air, horizontally across the treetops, vertically along the trunks, until the entire jungle is filled with color, like a ball pit filled with elongated balloons. A sloth looks like an upside-down carnival ride because of all the colored tubes of the algae and insects that live in its fur.

I feel how everything is interconnected, how each animal and plant is a small element in a complex interplay with a hidden mechanism.

I think I finally fell asleep. The next morning I wake up in my own bed and remain passive all day long. I feel empty, but also very lucid. A hollow glass version of myself. Nina visits me several times to see how I'm doing, reassures me, and tells me it's all part of the experience. She asks me to tell her what I experienced; right then it's still too early for me to write things down.

I didn't find the answer I was looking for, but I did find a deep understanding of the mutual relationships in the jungle, where every plant and animal depends on others, even if sometimes only to serve as food or pollination agents. The forest is so much more than a collection of trees and shrubs. It's a complex composition of living elements, each with its own appearance and behavior. I also have a clearer picture of myself. The direction I need to go, the task I can set myself.

August 5, 1980

Tomorrow we will visit Puerto Maldonado once again. The elections for governor of Madre de Dios province were won by the leftist candidate. He defeated the incumbent right-wing governor. Tomorrow morning he will be inaugurated and this is expected to be widely celebrated during the afternoon. He made several promises that are important for the area and the indigenous people.

The new governor has already announced that he is ordering an investigation into the dam project and various land expropriations by agricultural companies. It has already been established that some documents were forgeries.

August 6, 1980

Everything is broken, everything has been smashed to smithereens, the ridge of my house has been sawn in half and has fallen down, the camera lies in a myriad of pieces on the floor. The mosquito net and my clothes are in tatters. Even the drawers with the little plants next to the house are completely shattered. It is a miracle that the notebooks, my diaries, are still there. They were tucked under the mattress.

I was in the big city. When I returned, a few people were approaching me. They talked about armed men who had attacked the village at the time when many villagers were in Puerto Maldonado. Those who had remained behind in the village had been powerless.

Was it a targeted action against me? Or was my house just the first thing they had come across? After all, they had come through the forest, at the back of the village.

I am so incredibly tired. With difficulty I cleared my bed of dust
and shards. And replaced one leg of the bed as best I could with
a block of wood. I lay on the bed with my clothes on, staring at
the starry sky. I expected to fall asleep at any moment, but then
there was Nina insisting that I spend the night at her place.

August 7, 1980

I woke up early and am now sitting on Nina's porch with coffee
and my diaries, perhaps my only possessions that remained
intact.

I had a restless night and feel lousy. One negative thought after
the other goes through my mind. For the first time in a long
while, I feel tense. What am I going to do? Do I stay here or do I
go back to the Netherlands? What business do I have in the
Netherlands? What business do I have here? Will the new
governor keep his promises? In a few years, maybe everything
will be flooded here, and everyone will have moved elsewhere.
Isn't it a big joke? I come from a city that is yards below sea level
and now here, in the middle of the Amazon forest, I am being
driven out by the water, maybe?

The jungle won't reveal its secrets. No matter how much I
puzzle.
I learned all kinds of new things, discovered one thing after
another, but the jungle ultimately won and kept its mysteries.
And so it had all been in vain. I am unable to discover how new

trees grow from the Brazil nuts. They are buried, moved and sometimes forgotten by the agoutis, but they do not germinate. This is something the villagers told me months ago. The link that remains a secret is exactly what is so important for the incomes of the farming families. And ultimately for the survival of the forest.

August 8, 1980

Today we repaired my house. Half of the villagers helped out, and even a few relatives from outside the village joined in. This morning we selected a tree from the forest. It had a beautiful straight trunk with the right circumference for becoming the new ridge of the house. The trunk was cut to the required length in the jungle and stripped of its bark, after which we all worked together and brought the colossus to the village.

Nobody asked whether I was staying or not. The house needed to be repaired, that was all, and everyone thought that was self-evident. There was also little discussion. If there was any conversation, it was usually about completely unrelated things. Actually, everyone was quite cheerful, as if it concerned an annual maintenance job. My own mood is also slightly better again, although I still have no idea what I'm going to do.

The new ridge was lifted into place with manpower. The women from the village braided the rest of the roof. They used leaves of the *geonoma,* a low-growing palm tree, with long parallel leaves that made its branches very suitable for roofing. They told me that such a roof lasts several years after which it needs to be replaced.

I just stood there watching; they were so skilled at it. Years of experience. Again, this was done with little consultation with me or among themselves. A collective sense of what needed to be done.

August 10, 1980

I lost my necklace. The gold chain with the locket containing Gonny's picture. It probably happened while cutting down the tree or hauling the trunk. Twilight is already setting in and I am tired. Tomorrow I need to get back to the spot as soon as possible, before peccaries root up the soil, or a bird or monkey scurries off with the shiny object.

September 3, 1980

I have been sick for 3 weeks. Very likely it was *Chikungunya,* a nasty virus transmitted by mosquitoes. During the construction of the roof and ridge, I had probably paid too little attention to protective clothing.

I developed a high fever, with joint- and headaches. After a few days, I developed a rash. I had delirious dreams about giant agoutis and about Brazil nuts that I had to categorize. Over and over again. It seems that at one point I even stood half-naked in the grassy field, wildly gesticulating while redesigning the village.

Nina visited regularly and I vaguely remember a shaman as well. I was given an anti-inflammatory drug and heavy painkillers. The fever and rash are now gone, but the joint-ache is still there. Especially in my fingers.

September 4, 1980

I went back to where the tree had been cut down, looking for my necklace. While hauling away the tree trunk, I hadn't really paid any attention to the route we took through the forest, so I had to search quite a bit. I eventually recovered it, but much more than that. Finally the story has come full circle, and the story is so incredibly beautiful!

I wanted to go and look for the necklace early in the morning, but it ended up being mid-day.
Arriving at the sawed-off tree, I first searched the spot where I stood when the villagers were sawing. With a branch, I turned up the leaves on the ground. It was annoying that so much time had passed since I had lost the necklace.
Where the tree stood, an opening has appeared in the canopy and a bright shaft of sunlight replaced it. Insects fly around in

circles in the light. Such direct sunlight on the ground is a rarity in the dense jungle. Even in the middle of the day when the sun is high in the sky. At that moment I see something shiny. That's the necklace, I know. And a second later I see the small plants.

And then I understand. Right there and then my search has ended. A warm feeling surges through my body, a feeling of fulfilment, of completion.
In the sunlight, three small plants, pale yellow and green, have been working their way up through the soil and the dead leaves.

But all tree species look alike when they are so young. Even though I have grown Brazil nut plants myself, I am still not sure. This could be anything. I intuitively put the necklace in my pocket. I go down on my knees and push the brown leaves aside. I stick my fingers deep into the soggy soil. I need to be sure. I pull up a clod and let the soil fall through my fingers. What I am left with is the little plant with a long pale stem. And at the bottom of that stem there's a Brazil nut with its thin root.

As I feel the moisture from the ground permeating through the fabric at my knees I can see the whole story before me: the epiphytes in the tree attracting the male orchid bees, the females pollinating the blossom of the Brazil nut, after which the fruits grow, falling like cannon balls in the rainy season, the agoutis opening the fruits, eating the nuts, leaving only a few of them, and burying these leftovers far away from the tree, partially digging them up and burying them again further on in a shady spot, a stockpile that remains in place as if in a kind of hibernation. Until the moment when a fallen tree creates an opening in the canopy that allows sufficient sunlight to pass through.

That is the time when conditions are optimal: when the sun provides enough energy over an extended period of time to grow a tree, when a Brazil nut takes root, and a new tree emerges.

This is why the nuts in the containers next to my house germinated, while those in "my little garden" in the dark jungle did not.

But here and now, three little plants have sprouted in the forest. And one of them will triumph over the other two and grow to majestic heights, above all the other trees.

Epilogue

This is where my uncle's notes end. He continued to live in the Peruvian Amazon for a very long time, but he no longer wrote in his diary.

More and more frequently he was visited by biologists, ecologists, researchers and other curious people. Even after his death and after his personal belongings had been sent to the Netherlands, researchers sometimes stopped by to visit the village of Iyacu and Anton Smelt's former home.

He was buried in his "little garden" the patch of jungle where he conducted his research. Among the dormant Brazil nuts, under the paws of hungry agoutis. Pretty soon after that, Fundación Antón Smelt was established. This foundation provides information and education about the Amazon.

The import rules of the EEC (later EC and now EU) regarding carcinogenic aflatoxin have become increasingly strict. For all types of nuts, but also for other crops. These rules poses a real challenge for exporting countries.

The planned dam was never built. An investigation revealed a lot of corruption. Among other things, title deeds and cost-benefit calculations of the dam's power output had been tampered with. Some of those responsible were jailed. The companies involved had to pay hefty fines.

The new governor has implemented extensive regulations to protect the jungle. On September 4, 2000, the Tambopata area was declared a national park by President Alberto Fujimori. Finally not only the Brazil nut trees, but the entire forest where they grow is protected. For their economic importance, but also for the preservation of the indigenous culture.

Nina eventually returned to Cusco, where she is fighting for the rights of indigenous people, against the discrimination of the jungle population, and against illegal land expropriations. She has also worked at the university to assist in the development of a simple and inexpensive stove that burns on briquettes made from jungle waste that contains 80 percent Brazil nut shells.

Acknowledgement

Writing can be a long and lonely process. So I am glad that all the help I received along the way was not only valuable, but also extremely enjoyable. For this I would like to extend my special thanks to a number of people.

Stijn de Jong for his enthusiasm and detailed stories about his stay in the Amazon jungle.

Nienke Oostenbrink who was willing to share her knowledge and information about young Brazil nut trees with me.

Ella Huizinga and everyone else who makes "De Pijp" in Groningen, the Netherlands, such a great place to work.

Louis Stiller for his wide-ranging advice and decades of friendship.

Eisso Post for his extensive comments ranging from pointing out typos to asking overarching questions that get to the heart of this book.

My "reading group": Arnoud Warmerdam, Jaap van der Lee, Monique Jacobs and René Raap, all of whom made valuable suggestions, each in their own way.

My old school friend, the late Anton Valens, who, without ever knowing it himself, inspired my writing.

Koop Tissingh of A&E Translations for his excellent translation from Dutch to English.

Finally, all the writers, researchers and conservationists who show us the beauty, complexity and importance of the Amazon forest and all the other forests and woodlands on our vulnerable planet.